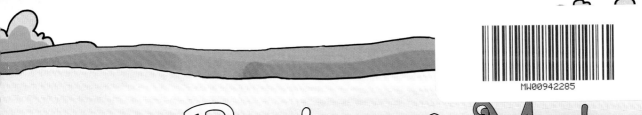

Paxton & Mali FIND THEIR BOAT

written by Dani Miller

Tate Publishing & Enterprises

Published by Tate Publishing & Enterprises, LLC
127 E. Trade Center Terrace | Mustang, Oklahoma 73064 USA
1.888.361.9473 | www.tatepublishing.com

Tate Publishing is committed to excellence in the publishing industry. The company reflects
the philosophy established by the founders, based on Psalm 68:11,
"The Lord gave the word and great was the company of those who published it."

Book design copyright © 2011 by Tate Publishing, LLC. All rights reserved.
Cover and interior design by Elizabeth M. Hawkins
Illustrations by Kurt Jones

Published in the United States of America
ISBN: 978-1-61346-289-8
Juvenile Fiction / Sports & Recreation / Water Sports
11.07.21

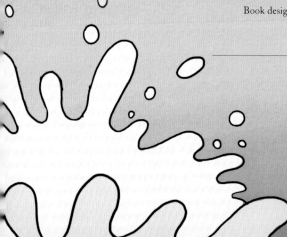

For my dad,

WHO TAUGHT ME HOW TO FISH

Paxton and his cousin Mali were playing with a toy boat in the backyard blue kiddie pool.

"Mali, what are we going to do today?" asked Paxton.

Smiling, Mali said, "We're going to find a fishing boat."

"Oh, fun!" Paxton said. "Let's go."

The children lay back on the grass on Paxton's frog pillow pet and put their hands behind their heads. They imagined they were standing in front of a huge sporting goods store.

There were several big boats outside of the entrance. One looked like a big pirate ship, and the other was a shiny speed boat. Paxton climbed into the pirate ship and imagined he was the captain looking for lost treasure. Mali jumped into the speed boat and made engine noises while she pretended she was pulling a water skier behind her.

Paxton and Mali stepped inside the big sporting goods store with their pet frog on a leash. "Let's go find a boat, Mali," Paxton said. "Okay," Mali agreed.

"Look at all the colors we have to choose from," Mali said. "There are red, yellow, blue, and—look over here—orange, purple, and green!" shouted Paxton.

"Paxton, look at this one! It's red and purple with sparkles."
Mali pointed to a candy apple red and purple metallic boat.
"Wow," Paxton said. "Nice!"

Paxton climbed up into the driver's seat and pretended he was reeling in the biggest bass fish he had ever seen while Mali grabbed an imaginary net to pull the fish inside the boat. Their pet frog sat at the top of the boat's large motor.

"I think we should get this one, Paxton," Mali said.

"Yes," said Paxton.

"This is it!" Mali said. "We need these life jackets for our new boat, to keep us safe in the water. Look, a purple one for me and a red one for you—they match the boat!"

Paxton picked up a huge, black fishing net and exclaimed, "We need one of these for all the fish we are going to catch." Paxton imagined he was netting a massive catfish.

Mali came around the corner of the aisle with a shopping basket, filling the cart with colorful lures, hooks, and fishing accessories.

"We need all this to catch big fish?" Paxton asked Mali.

"You have a lot to learn, Paxton." Mali giggled.

Paxton and Mali were back at home in the backyard.

"Time to come in for dinner, Paxton," said Paxton's mom from inside the house.

Paxton looked over at Mali. "So what are we going to do tomorrow, Mali?"

Mali said, "We are going to the lake to try out our new boat, of course."

e|LIVE

---

listen|imagine|view|experience

AUDIO BOOK DOWNLOAD INCLUDED WITH THIS BOOK!

In your hands you hold a complete digital entertainment package. In addition to the paper version, you receive a free download of the audio version of this book. Simply use the code listed below when visiting our website. Once downloaded to your computer, you can listen to the book through your computer's speakers, burn it to an audio CD or save the file to your portable music device (such as Apple's popular iPod) and listen on the go!

How to get your free audio book digital download:

1. Visit www.tatepublishing.com and click on the e|LIVE logo on the home page.
2. Enter the following coupon code:
   af06-2587-62b1-d77d-f1f4-1661-f75e-0abc
3. Download the audio book from your e|LIVE digital locker and begin enjoying your new digital entertainment package today!